OLIVER FIBBS
AND THE ABOMINABLE SNOW PENGUIN

Steve Hartley is many things: author, astronaut, spy, racing-car driver, trapeze-artist and vampire-hunter. His hobbies include puddle-diving and hamster-wrestling and he was voted `Coolest Dude of the Year' for five years running by *Seriously Cool* magazine. Steve is 493 years old, lives in a golden palace on top of a dormant volcano in Lancashire and never, EVER, tells fibs. You can find out more about Steve on his extremely silly website: www.stevehartley.net

Books by Steve Hartley

The DANNY BAKER RECORD BREAKER series

The World's Biggest Bogey

The World's Awesomest Air-Barf

The World's Loudest Armpit Fart

The World's Stickiest Earwax

The World's Itchiest Pants

The World's Windiest Baby

The Wibbly Wobbly Jelly Belly Flop

The OLIVER FIBBS series

Oliver Fibbs: Attack of the Alien Brain

Oliver Fibbs and the Giant Boy-Munching Bugs

Oliver Fibbs and the Abominable Snow Penguin

www.stevehartley.net

OLIVER FIBBS

AND THE ABOMINABLE SNOW PENGUIN

STEVE HARTLEY

ILLUSTRATED BY BERNICE LUM

MACMILLAN CHILDREN'S BOOKS

First published 2014 by Macmillan Children's Books
a division of Macmillan Publishers Limited
20 New Wharf Road, London N1 9RR
Basingstoke and Oxford
Associated companies throughout the world
www.panmacmillan.com

ISBN 978-1-4472-2028-2

1 3 5 7 9 8 6 4 2

A CIP catalogue record for this book is available from
the British Library.

Printed and bound by CPI Group (UK) Ltd, Croydon CRO 4YY

For Rosie, Connie and Louise,
and for Sarah Manson,
with many, many thanks

(SH)

For Charles, much love

(BL)

I'M OLIVER

Hi! I'm Oliver Ranulph Templeton Tibbs, mild-mannered comic-reader and **EXTREME PIZZA-EATER.**

Also known as Oliver 'Fibbs', just because I tell people I'm

DABMAN, the Daring and Brave, dashing and bold DEFENDER OF PLANET EARTH (D.O.P.E.).

Meet my Super And Special family:

Mum, Charlotte Pomeroy Templeton Tibbs, is a life-saving brain surgeon.

Dad, Granville Fitzwilliam Templeton Tibbs, is an award-winning architect.

My big twin sisters, Emma Letitia and Gemma Darcy Templeton Tibbs, go to the National Ballet Academy: ballet, ballet, ballet – it's all they talk about.

Then there's my little brother, Algy – Algernon Montgomery Templeton Tibbs. He's

a maths genius, chess champion and King of Sneakiness.

And how could I forget Constanza, our Italian nanny? She's a bit dizzy, but she gets me.

At school, I've got my best friend Peaches Mazimba on my side. She's the most sensible person *ever*, so I've recruited her to be a D.O.P.E. like me: she's `**Captain Common Sense**´.

Unfortunately, I've got the Super And Special Gang against me:

Bobby Bragg can break bricks in half with his bare

hands. Aka `the Show-off', he has the Power to **BORE PEOPLE STIFF.**

Hattie Hurley is a Spelling Bee Cheerleading Champion. Aka `the Spell Queen', she has the Power of **Big Words.**

Toby Hadron is a science whizz. Aka `the Boffin', he has the Power of Inventing **REALLY SCARY STUFF.**

And finally there's my teacher, Miss Wilkins, Keeper of the **SHINE TIME** Points, and dispenser of detentions, especially when she thinks I'm telling **FIBS** – but as I keep telling her (and everyone else): they're not **FIBS**, they're stories!

CHAPTER 1

DEEP THOUGHT

The human race was doomed. A meteor the size of Mount Kilimanjaro was hurtling straight for the Earth. When it crashed, tons of dust would be thrown into the atmosphere, blocking out the sun for a hundred years. The global temperature would plummet. Millions of people would die!

There were less than two minutes to impact . . .

`Oliver, have you got wedged in the toilet

seat again?' asked Dad, knocking urgently on the bathroom door.

'He's been in there for over an hour,' I heard my little brother, Algy, say.

I sighed. Was there nowhere in this house where I could sit and have a nice, quiet read of my **Agent Q** comic?

'No, everything's OK,' I replied. 'I'm just . . . thinking.'

'*Really?*' said Dad, not even *trying* to hide the note of **SURPRISE** in his voice. 'What are you thinking about?'

'Oh, you know: life, the universe, and . . . stuff.'

'Excellent news!' he exclaimed. 'Algy, leave

your brother in peace – he Needs To Think.'
(That's how he said it, like each word had a
capital letter.)

'But I need to pee,' complained Algy.

'Then go downstairs.'

I heard my little brother stomp away,
growling and grumbling.

'You have a good think, Oliver,' Dad shouted
to me through the door. 'Take as long as you
need. Just remember that your uncle Sir
Randolph is coming for lunch. He wants to say
goodbye before he sets off on his expedition to
Amble Across the Antarctic.'

The creaking floorboards along the landing
told me that Dad was striding off to his office.
Finally, I could get to the end of *Agent Q and
the* Arctic Blast.

3

The meteor crashing towards the Earth was being controlled by evil Russian billionaire Boris Popov, the owner of Popov's Pants, who had made his fortune selling woolly underpants with the catchphrase: `A warm bottom is a happy bottom´.

A WARM BOTTOM...

IS A HAPPY BOTTOM!

But now the globe was getting warmer, and so many people had stopped buying Boris's snuggly underwear that he was losing millions of roubles every day. When the meteor struck and the world froze, Popov's Pants would be back in business.

Q had discovered the villain's secret headquarters in the icy wastes of northern

Siberia, but when he got there the building was deserted. As Q stood in the empty control room, surrounded by humming computers, glowing buttons and flashing lights, Boris Popov's face appeared on a huge screen . . .

I closed the comic and sighed. I wanted to be Daring and Brave like **Agent Q**, but I was stuck with being **Dull And Boring.** I spent my whole life drowning in an ocean of Super And Special people, competing with my **BRILLIANT** family at home, and all the **BRILLIANT** kids at school.

I opened the toilet door, and cried out in alarm.

Mum and Dad were waiting outside, grinning at me like I was the cutest puppy in Cutepuppyland. Mum was holding a thick, heavy book in front of her like a shield.

I snapped the comic out of sight behind my back and gave them my best innocent smile.

'This is great news, Oliver,' Mum said. 'You've decided to start thinking.'

'Er . . . yes,' I replied. 'I thought it was about time I did.'

'Maybe you're going to be a great philosopher, and have . . . **Big Ideas**,' she said, holding out the book she was carrying as though it was a precious ancient relic.

The title shone out from the shiny black cover in fancy silver writing: *The Deepest Thoughts of the Biggest Brains of All Time.*

The Deepest Thoughts of the Biggest Brains of All Time

'All human wisdom is in here,' she added.

Here we go again, I thought. Another big, complicated book to read, when all I actually want to read is a comic.

I let my **Agent Q** story fall quietly behind the toilet door, and took the monster book from Mum's hands. It was so heavy I nearly dropped it.

'Wow! Thanks, Mum!' I exclaimed, and I meant

it too: this was going to be an excellent book to hide my comics inside. 'I'll make a start on it now.'

Dad puffed out his chest, his big daft grin spreading even wider across his face. 'That's my boy,' he said, his eyes glistening with tears. 'Take your time, Oliver. Take as long as you need.'

I stepped back into the toilet. As I slowly closed the door, my parents continued to stand there, beaming happily.

I picked up *Agent Q and the* Arctic **Blast**, and slipped it inside the great big book of deep thoughts: it was a perfect fit. Opening my comic at page one, I started to read the story all over again.

CHAPTER 2

A HERO IN THE HOUSE

Just as I got to the end of the **Agent Q** adventure for the second time, I heard the yippy~yappy bark of a tiny dog downstairs.

'Poochie!' I cried.

'WHERE'S OLLIE?' bellowed my uncle, Sir Randolph Maxwell Templeton Tibbs.

Uncle Sir Randolph was Dad's older brother

and a famous explorer, or 'Professional Wanderer', as he liked to be called. He was THE superstar in my family of superstars, the only one who'd been knighted by the Queen. Even my **BRILLIANT** brain surgeon mum and my **BRILLIANT** architect dad spoke about my uncle with awe in their voices. He had *real*

adventures that could have come from the pages of a comic book. He wasn't just cool, he was arctic.

I slammed closed *The Deepest Thoughts of the Biggest Brains of All Time*, and ran downstairs to greet my favourite relative. He stood in the hallway surrounded by the rest of my family, but seemed to tower above them all, filling the space like a huge grizzly bear.

Great plumes of black hair, flecked with long streaks of grey, billowed up from his head, cascaded down from his chin, and exploded out from his tangly eyebrows, so that from a distance, his whole head appeared to be SMOKING. A thin, white scar slashed diagonally across his forehead, the result of a near-miss from a bandit's arrow in the Sahara Desert.

Uncle Sir Randolph saw me and his face lit up in a dazzling, toothy white smile. `THERE HE IS!' he roared, and held up his left hand in greeting.

We all stared at it, transfixed by the
missing tip of his index finger, **BITTEN** off by
a mountain lion in the Rocky Mountains.

`Give me four and a half!' cried my Uncle, and his **THUNDEROUS** laughter rumbled through the house.

I leaped to my feet and smacked his hand with mine. He picked me up, hurled me towards the ceiling, then caught me as if I was as light as a beach ball.

All this time, Poochie darted around our feet, yapping excitedly. My uncle's dog was a miniature version of him: a tiny, noisy, puff-ball of frizzy grey-black hair.

`Be quiet, Poochie!' yelled Uncle Sir Randolph,

then **ROARED** with laughter as the dog completely ignored him, yipping and scampering around the hallway.

'I hope Constanza has made her delicious meatballs for lunch,' he **BOOMED**, scooping the dog up in one of his massive hands. 'I need all the energy I can get where I'm going.'

'I make them extra beefy, Signore Randolph,' replied our Italian nanny, 'to keep you warm on the snow.'

'Excellent!' bellowed my uncle, and strode into the dining room, his huge, broad shoulders brushing the doorframes as he passed through.

'I read in the paper that you've won *another* architecture award, Granville,' he said, slapping Dad on the shoulder as they sat down at the table.

'Yes,' replied Dad, 'for designing the new

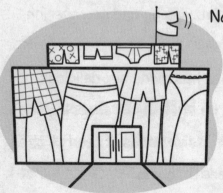

National Museum of Underpants in Wakefield.'

Uncle Sir Randolph turned to Mum. 'And, Charlotte, I hear you've just done a brain operation on pop star Justin Peeper. I didn't even know he had a brain!'

As we laughed, he looked across the table at my twin sisters Emma and Gemma. They hung on every word my uncle spoke, their cheeks bright pink, and eyes shining.

'How's the ballet dancing going, girls?' he asked them.

`We're in the National Teen Ballet Company,´ said Emma.

`We passed our Advanced Grade exams with Distinction,´ added Gemma.

`Algy won the European Junior Chess Championships,´ said Dad, `and Oliver . . .´ He paused and frowned slightly, as he realized that I hadn't done anything Super And Special to brag about.

`Oliver's going to be a great philosopher,´ said Mum.

My uncle gazed at us all for a moment, and shook his head. `What an amazing family I've got!´ he said.

`Tell us about the time you survived an **avalanche** in the Himalayas by body-surfing down the snow in your sleeping bag,

Uncle Sir Randolph,' pleaded Algy.

This was my little brother's favourite story, and as we ate lunch we made my uncle tell us more tales of his adventures, even though we'd heard them a hundred times before.

'I need to use the little boys' room,' announced Uncle Sir Randolph, when we'd finished eating. 'I'll just explore upstairs and see if you've moved it.'

'You'll have to use the bathroom downstairs,' said Mum. 'The toilet upstairs belongs to Oliver now.'

'It's where he does his thinking,' explained Dad.

'Well, I'm desperate for a "think",' chuckled Uncle Sir Randolph. 'So, if you'll excuse me, I'm off to the downstairs Thinking Room!'

He returned a couple of minutes later carrying a massive rucksack.

`I have a special job for each one of you kids while I'm away,´ he announced. `Girls, I want you to look after Poochie.´

The twins squealed with delight, and both dived for the tiny grey hairball, who was fast asleep under the table.

`Come on, Gem,´ cried Emma. `Let's play with Poochie!´

`I've got a better idea, Em,´ said Gemma. `Let's *pamper* Poochie!´

They rushed from the dining room, fussing over the poor, startled dog.

Uncle Sir Randolph rummaged in his rucksack,

pulled out a large snow globe and handed it to Algy. Inside, a family of plastic penguins stood like statues on a **JAGGED** pretend iceberg that towered above a painted blue-grey sea.

'Explorers are terribly superstitious,' he said, giving the globe a quick shake to start a white plastic blizzard swirling around the penguins. 'I want you to shake this

globe every morning and every night to make sure I have good luck. Do you promise to do that?'

'I promise,' whispered Algy.

My uncle presented me with a black satellite phone. `Ollie, while I'm on my expedition, I want you to be my base-camp. Your codename is "**LIFELINE**". My codename is "**SUPER SNOWMAN**". I'll phone you from the Antarctic every day and give you an update on my progress.´

`Wow,´ I breathed, turning the heavy phone over in my hands.

Uncle Sir Randolph put his hand on my shoulder and frowned, his grey eyes staring into mine as he handed me a blood-red envelope with the words "**CODE RED RESCUE PLAN**" written in big capital letters on the front.

'If anything goes wrong,' he continued, tapping the envelope with the stump of his **BITTEN**-off finger, 'we activate **CODE RED.** It'll be up to you to get help.'

'Wow,' I breathed again.

My uncle frowned, and stared out of the window. 'There was a time when my beloved Bunty was my **LIFELINE,**' he murmured, his eyes filling with tears. 'But then ...'

He shook his head as though waking from a dream, then slapped me hard on the arm, rocketing me across the room. 'Are you up to the job?' he roared.

'I won't let you down, Uncle Sir Randolph,' I replied.

Wait until my class hears about this, I thought. Bobby Bragg

24

will be so green with envy he'll
look just like the hideous warty
Toadman in **Agent Q and the
Slimeball Peril.**

CHAPTER 3

SHOW AND TELL

As Constanza drove us to school on Monday morning, I tingled with excitement at the thought of doing **SHOW AND TELL**. I usually call it PAIN AND TORTURE time because everything I do, apart from my *FIBS* – I mean stories – is *totally* **Dull And Boring**. But for once I couldn't wait to stand up and tell my schoolmates all about my Super And Special role in Uncle Sir Randolph's expedition. Just my

luck, today I was the last to be dropped off,
as we took Algy to university, and the twins to
their ballet school.

I hurried into the classroom and sat down.
As Miss Wilkins began to go through the register,
my tummy fluttered with nerves as I got ready
to tell the class about Uncle Sir Randolph, and
show them the satellite phone he'd given me.
Surely none of the Super And Special Kids would
have something more interesting to talk about
than this?

Wrong!

Bobby Bragg had
taken up ice-skating
a month before, and
announced that he'd
got so good at it that

the Riptorn Assassins Junior ice-hockey
squad – the best, and hardest, team in the
country – had already signed him to play for
them next season.

The other kids went, `Oooooooo.´

`How **exciting**!´ said Miss Wilkins.

Toby Hadron, the school science whizz,
had invented a **SNOW**-machine. He wheeled in
a metal box with hoses, power leads and pipes
running from it. A short, wide tube, like the
barrel of a cannon, stuck out at an angle from
the top of the box. Toby flicked a switch, and
snowflakes were blasted from the end of the
tube, turning the air white.

`Stop!´ cried Miss Wilkins as tiny crystal
flecks settled gently on our heads. `How magical!
At lunchtime, why don´t we see if your machine

can cover the
playground in snow.´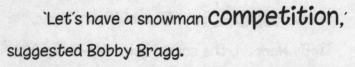

`Let´s make
snowmen,´ said my best
friend Peaches Mazimba.

`Let´s have a snowman **competition**,´
suggested Bobby Bragg.

`Excellent idea!´ said the teacher as a
babble of **excited** chatter filled the
classroom.

Peaches leaned over to me. `Let´s be a
team!´ she said.

When everyone had calmed down, Hattie
Hurley stood up with her red, white and blue
pom-poms at the ready. She told the class
that she´d started her own dictionary of **Big
Words,** to help her and the National Super-

Spellers Cheerleading Team defend their title of World Spelling Bee Cheerleading Champions.

`I'm only including words that have at least eight letters in them,´ she said. `Like "aardvark", "abominable", and "antihistamine"!´

`How admirable,´ said Miss Wilkins.

`A-D-M-I-R-A-B-L-E!´ spelled Hattie, kicking her legs high into the air with each letter, and waving the pom-poms above her head.

`Correct!´ laughed the teacher, and we all clapped.

Peaches is normally **Dull And Boring** like me, but she'd made a lampshade out of green and red recycled milk-bottle tops. It was fantastic.

'How unusual!' said Miss Wilkins.

Then Melody Nightingale sang a song inspired by Toby's snow machine, called, 'There's No Business Like **SNOW** Business!'

'How lovely,' sighed Miss Wilkins.

Eventually it was my turn. I stood up, and began.

'My uncle is Sir Randolph Maxwell Templeton Tibbs, the world famous explorer.'

The class went, 'Oooooooooooo!'

(It was at least two oo's bigger than Bobby Bragg got.)

'He's going on a single-handed Amble Across the Antarctic.'

Before the class could make any sound, Bobby Bragg shouted, `Liar! Liar! Pants on fire!´

`That's enough, Bobby,´ scolded Miss Wilkins. `I saw Sir Randolph on the ten o'clock news last night, so I know Oliver's not telling **FIBS** this time.´

`That's right, miss,´ I said. I reached into my bag, and slowly revealed the heavy black satellite phone. `My uncle's going to call me every day on this, to give me an update on his expedition. I've got a special codename: ˝**LIFELINE**˝.´

The kids went, `Ahhhhhhh.´

I held up the big red envelope. `And if he gets in trouble, I have special instructions to get help: the ˝**CODE RED RESCUE PLAN**˝.´

The kids went, 'Wooooooowww!'

Bragg pulled a face at me, but said nothing. It was going better than I could have hoped.

But then Miss Wilkins spoilt everything.

'I've got an idea!' she said. 'We can use your uncle's expedition for a class project on the Antarctic. Some of you can research the animals, or the science and geography, or the history of polar exploration.'

Miss Wilkins was on a roll now.

'We can think about how Sir Randolph will survive on his expedition. What food will he take? What clothes will he need?'

'How will he go to the toilet?' wondered Leon Curley.

'Maybe he wears a big nappy!' shouted Bobby Bragg.

The class laughed, while I tried not to think about it.

Too late!

`Maybe Oliver can ask his uncle if he'll talk to us about his adventure when he gets back. Then he can answer all our questions!' said Miss Wilkins, clapping her hands and giving a little squeal of excitement. `For the next three weeks, we won't have SHOW AND TELL. Instead, you can all give updates on your Antarctic projects. You can work on them in class, do homework each night, then prepare your presentations

each weekend. Won't that be fun?'

All the Super And Special Kids went, 'Nooooooooooooooooooooooooooooooooooo!'

Miss Wilkins thought they were all joking and laughed.

But it was no joke. Just like the fire-eyed demons in *Agent Q and the* HOTHOUSE HORROR, the hot, angry eyes of the **SAS** GANG were fixed on me, willing my body to melt and

turn into a huge, sloppy blob of Oliver Tibbs.

'I've not got time for homework!' hissed Bobby Bragg as I sat down at my table.

'I'm doing ice-hockey training with the Riptorn Assassins next weekend.'

`And I'm at a spelling-bee camp,´ added Hattie Hurley.

`And I'm creating an iceberg in the bath,´ complained Toby Hadron.

Bobby snarled. `Thanks for nothing, Fibbs!´

Peaches didn't seem to mind. `This is so **exciting**!´ she said as I sat down. `I'm going to make you a special holster out of a recycled cushion cover, so you can carry the phone around on a belt.

After lunch, everyone hurried outside, as Toby's machine covered the entire playground in a thick layer of **SNOW**, like icing on a cake. Fine flakes swirled around in the air. I looked up, but was dazzled by the sun, shining in a cloudless blue sky.

Half an hour later, the playground was crowded with snowmen, snow-women, snow-cats and snow-dogs. Peaches and I had made a snow-octopus, and I have to say it was pretty amazing. None of the sculptures were as amazing as the gigantic snow-penguin Bobby, Toby and Hattie had built in the middle of the playground. They won the competition easily.

Toby's snow-machine kept chucking out streams of dancing white flakes and, while it was melting fast in the sun, there was still enough snow left for a mass snowball fight before we went inside.

Bobby Bragg ambushed Peaches, shoving a handful of **FREEZING** slush down her neck.

`Ollie, help!' shouted Peaches.

I began to run towards them, but slipped and fell – **SPLAT** – in the snow. I skidded and slid helplessly, only stopping when I clattered into the back of Peaches's legs. Arms flailing, she tumbled backwards over me and sat down heavily in the lake of grey slush that now covered the playground.

`Cold, wet knickers,' she moaned. `Not nice.'

`I'm going to be soaking for the rest of the morning,' I complained to Peaches.

`I'm not,' she said, pulling a spare pair of pants and socks from her Eco Warrior shoulder bag. `I always carry spares, just in case.'

`What, in case you sit in a puddle of artificial snow?'

39

Peaches just smiled and shrugged. `Well, it happened, didn't it?´

Sometimes, even **DAB**MAN can't argue with Captain Common Sense!

CHAPTER 4

PROJECT ANTARCTICA

A week later, there was a real buzz of **excitement** in the class when I stood up and told everyone that the expedition was under way. Uncle Sir Randolph had parachuted on to the ice (how awesome is *that*?) and transmitted his first position.

43

I proudly stuck a red pin in the map of Antarctica on the wall at the back of the class to mark where he was.

`Tell us more about your famous uncle, Oliver,´ said Miss Wilkins. `Tell us about the places he's been and the adventures he's had.´

`He's explored all over the world,´ I began.

I counted them off on my fingers. `When he **STROLLED** across the Sahara, he was attacked by bandits and found the lost pyramid of King Tutti-frutti.´

The class went, `Ooooooooooo!´

`And when he **HIKED** up the Himalayas he survived an avalanche and found the lair of the legendary Not Yeti.´

The class went, `Ahhhhhhh!´

`And when he **PADDLED** across the Pacific

looking for the buried treasure of the fearsome pirate Captain Bluenose, he ran out of water and had to drink his own wee!´

The class went, `Eeeewwwwww!´

`In the Rockies, he fought off mountain lions and found the secret gold mine of Grumpy Gordon McGrundy.´

The class went, `Woooooowwww!´

`And when he tiptoed through the tulips, he got stuck in the slime-trap of the Dutch Assassin Slug that was guarding the Magical Dancing Clogs of the ancient Queen of Cleves.´

Some of the kids went, `Oooooooooo,´ a few went, `Ahhhhhhhh,´ and the rest

went, 'Wowwwwwww!' so the sound came out as a *seriously* impressed-sounding 'Woooaahhhhooooooowwwwow'.

I thought, Thanks, Uncle Sir Randolph.

'He's a rubbish explorer,' shouted Bobby Bragg. 'He always gets lost and has to be rescued!'

Actually, my uncle *did* have a habit of wandering off in the wrong direction, but I wasn't going to let Bobby make fun of him.

`*Real* heroes don't care if they get lost,´ I countered. `And anyway, sometimes Uncle Sir Randolph gets lost because he follows the directions on his magical wooden compass.´

`Joke! Joke! Your nose is broke!´ sang Bobby.

`There's no such thing as magic,´ said Toby Hadron. `Just science.´

`It's real,´ I told them. `One day, not long after he'd decided to become an explorer, my uncle got lost trying to find the gift-shop at the Royal Society of Wanderers. He wandered into

47

a dark room full of **STRANGE** objects from around the world. In the centre of the room, sitting on a velvet cushion, was a battered, ancient wooden compass . . .

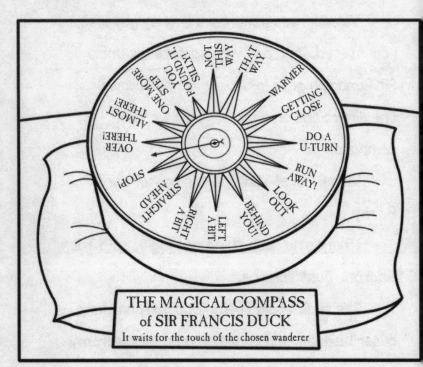

THE MAGICAL COMPASS
of SIR FRANCIS DUCK
It waits for the touch of the chosen wanderer

`As Sir Randolph picked up the compass, it began to glow with a **SPOOKY** light,´ I said. `The needle sprang to life, swinging and circling around the face. Then the compass spoke, its deep voice echoing around the vast room.

`That's how Uncle Sir Randolph discovers all these legendary places when he goes wandering,´ I explained.

`How unlikely!´ said Miss Wilkins, smiling as I

sat back down in my seat. `Oliver, I'd like you to give us all a daily update on your uncle's progress. It'll feel like we are almost on the expedition with him: trudging through blizzards, climbing steep **JAGGED** ice cliffs, huddling in a flimsy tent as an icy gale howls outside!'

If only that's what actually happened . . .

Every night, `**SUPER SNOWMAN**' phoned me on the satellite phone with a progress report and, every morning, I stood up in front of the class, and gave them the update.

Monday: `Walked thirteen kilometres. It snowed.'

Tuesday: `Walked nine and a half kilometres. It snowed.'

Wednesday: `Walked five kilometres. It snowed a bit more.'

Thursday: `Walked seven and a quarter kilometres. It snowed a bit less.´

The reaction of the other kids got worse each day.

On Monday, they were sniggering.

On Tuesday, they were shaking their heads.

On Wednesday, they were rolling their eyes.

On Thursday, they were **yawning.**

The trouble was, while my snow reports were getting more and more **Dull And Boring,** the rest of the class was doing projects that were getting more and more Super And Special.

Melody Nightingale showed us a picture of a **COLOSSAL** squid that lives deep in the Southern Ocean around the Antarctic. She said it grows to about 14 metres long, has got the biggest eyes of any animal on earth (about 40 centimetres across!) and long tentacles with massive suckers on the end to catch its prey.

'How scary!' said Miss Wilkins.

Hattie Hurley told us that her favourite Antarctic words were 'circumpolar', which means  'around the pole', and 'phytoplankton', which is the name for all the tiny plants that live in the sea.

'How informative!' said Miss Wilkins.

Leon Curley told us that Antarctica is covered in ice over one and a half kilometres thick, and the temperature once dropped to minus 89.2 degrees Celsius.

'How shiver-some!' said Miss Wilkins.

Then Millie Dangerfield showed us a
map of the Antarctic with great patches
coloured in red around the edge. 'Global
warming is making huge chunks of ice as big as
islands fall off and melt,' she cried. 'But, if all
the ice melts, the sea-level will rise, and we'll all
be drowned!'

She squeaked like a terrified gerbil, and
ran back to her seat.

'How alarming!' said Miss Wilkins.

Peaches was studying penguins (her
favourite animal). Pea told us that there are
about nineteen different types of penguins,
and that they only live in the southern part of
the world, not the north. She said the emperor

penguin is the biggest (over one metre tall),
and the fairy penguin is the smallest (about 30
centimetres tall).

She was wearing a pair of black wellington
boots with curving cardboard claws stuck on
the toes. 'I'm making an emperor penguin
suit,' she explained, 'but so far I've only done
the feet.'

'How
realistic!' said
Miss Wilkins.
Bobby
Bragg stood
up next.
'Killer whales
are the best
animals in the

Antarctic,' he said. 'They've got HUGE sharp teeth and they eat penguins. Leopard seals eat penguins too. And big birds called giant petrels eat penguin chicks.'

Peaches glared at him, and the class went, 'Awwwwww.'

'How gruesome!' said Miss Wilkins.

Bobby puffed up his shoulders. 'Nothing would eat me, miss,' he said. 'If I came face to face with a killer whale, I'd chop it in the fins – SMACK! – and kick it in the flippers! – POW!' Then he did a karate demonstration (as usual).

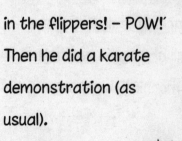

I was dreading Friday's project time, but then on Thursday night things got even worse. My uncle phoned me and said, `Hello, **LIFELINE**, **SUPER SNOWMAN** here! Walked ten and three-quarter kilometres today! It snowed. Saw a penguin . . . (crackle). It was . . . (crackle) . . . and . . . (crackle-crackle) . . . but then . . . (screeeeeeeeeeeech).´

Silence.

I pressed a few random buttons, but the phone was as dead as my Antarctic project. I stared at it, willing my uncle to call, but there was nothing. I tried to call him again before I went to school the next morning, but I just got crackles and hissing.

What was I going to tell my class? I didn't even have **Dull And Boring** stuff to report: I had Zip. Zero. Nothing.

As I stood up, many of them were grinning already, getting ready to burst into laughter at my latest **Dull And Boring** instalment. This was just like my normal **SHOW AND TELL** time. I know I shouldn't have done it, but it was as though my mouth had a life of its own. I couldn't stop myself. The words just tumbled out.

I thought, **WHAT IF** . . . the crackles and screeches I heard over the phone were actually the sound of some horrible ice **CREATURES** that were attacking my uncle?

`Just as Uncle Sir Randolph started to give me his latest report last night, I heard a terrifying shrieking noise . . .´

Toby Hadron frowned. `It's a scientific fact that there are no ants at the South Pole.´

`Why do you think it's called *Ant-arctica?´* I asked.

`The word means "opposite the Arctic",´ explained Hattie.

`That's what everyone thinks,´ I argued. `But the name *actually* means "land of the Arctic ants".´

`That sounds right,´ said Peaches, trying to help me out.

`Now, Oliver . . .´ said Miss Wilkins.

`Arctic ants are a legendary species of insect with pointy **POISONOUS** pincers, and hairy feet to keep their toes warm in the **SNOW**,´ I went on quickly. `They live in massive burrows hundreds of metres below the ice, and hunt whales, and walruses and . . . wanderers.´

A few of the class were smiling at me, but some, like Millie Dangerfield and Leon Curley, sat forward on their chairs, listening intently.

`When they go hunting, millions of ants wait at the edge of the ice and rub their back legs

59

together to make a loud chirruping sound. Seals and other sea creatures are hypnotized by the strange music, and when they poke their noses out of the water the ants swarm over them . . .´

I heard Millie gasp.

`Then the ants drag their prey on to the ice, and start munching,´ I continued. `So I knew my uncle was in big trouble . . .´

'What's happened to him, Oliver?' asked Millie. 'Is he all right?'

'I didn't know,' I replied. 'But I had to find out.' I stuck a pin in the map to show my uncle's last known position. 'This was a job for someone **Dashing And Brave, Daring And Bold**. This was a job for . . .

*DAB*MAN!'

Millie and Leon cheered.

Bobby Bragg groaned. '*FIB* Alert! *FIB* Alert! Tibbs has got a girly skirt!'

'Go for it, Ollie!' laughed Jamie Ryder.

'This is impossible,' said Toby Hadron.

'Antarctica's thousands of miles away – it takes weeks to get there.'

Toby was right: how *could* **DAB**MAN get to the Antarctic in seconds? Think, think, think! Then I remembered the lucky snow globe my uncle had given to Algy. **WHAT IF . . . ?**

HE SWIRLS IT, AND DISAPPEARS . . .
THEN REAPPEARS ON THE ICE.

A HEAT-RAY PULSES OUT FROM DABMAN'S HOT
PANTS AND MELTS THE ICE IN FRONT OF THE ANTS.

SUDDENLY, A GIANT SQUID BURSTS THROUGH THE HOLE IN THE ICE. THE ANTS
DROP SIR RANDOLPH AND SCATTER.

I paused, and gazed around the class. Everyone was silent, gripped by my story, except Bobby Bragg, who pretended to fall asleep and snore.

`There was only one way you can say thanks to a giant squid when he's just saved your life: give him a Snik-Snak chocolate bar.´

'It's a good thing **DABMAN** saved the day once again,' said Miss Wilkins. 'Otherwise, the expedition would have been over, and we'd have had to cancel all your project homework over the weekend.'

Then she gave me a playtime detention for **FIBBING**.

So at playtime I sat on my own in the classroom and wrote down my ant-attack tale as Miss Wilkins cut out paper snowflakes to hang up around the classroom, to give it a **FROSTY** feeling for our project.

At the end of the day, Constanza was nine minutes late picking me up. '*Mamma mia! Tragedia!* Emma tears her tutu, and Gemma loses her leotard. Boo-hoo! It is end of world, I think!'

Miss Wilkins took her to one side, and they

whispered to each other. I caught a few words: `ants´, `snowflake´, `hero´ and `plum pudding´.

Constanza tutted and shook her head at me. `Sir Randolph is a hero,´ she said as we walked back to the car. `You have no fib with him.´

`They're not **FIBS**, Constanza – they're stories,´ I reminded her.

`*Cattivo!*´ she replied. That's one of the few Italian words I know, because she says it all the time. It means `bad boy!´

The twins were slumped in the back seat, their eyes and faces red from sobbing.

`Madame Picamole will mark us down on

care of equipment,' blubbed Emma.

'And Eugenia Lovelace will get a higher mark than us,' sobbed Gemma.

'Whaaaaaaaaaaaa!' they bawled.

Algy rolled his eyes and grinned a naughty grin. I knew that look. What had my sneaky little brother been up to this time?

'You think you've got problems,' I yelled at them to make myself heard over their miserable wailing.

As we drove home, I stared out of the window. If only Uncle Sir Randolph WOULD get attacked by vicious Arctic ants, I thought, then I wouldn't have to make up stories.

CHAPTER 5

JINXED!

After supper, I told my family about the satellite phone not working.

`All sorts of things can affect radio signals,´ explained Algy. `Like bad weather, where you're standing and which way you point the phone. Try pointing it south towards the Antarctic. Also, the signal might be stronger in different rooms. You could even try using your body as a big aerial!´

So I roamed around the house, and
eventually managed to get the phone to work
in my Thinking Room by holding it upside down
and standing on my head in the bathtub with my
right foot sticking out of the bathroom window.

`Come in, **SUPER SNOWMAN**,´ I shouted
into the phone.

Uncle Sir Randolph´s voice was crackly and
faint. `Hello, **LIFELINE!**´ he answered. `Good to

hear from you at last . . . (hissssssssss) . . .
These phones are a nuisance . . . (crickle-
crick-crackle) . . . Are you ready for my Friday
update?´

`Have you seen any Arctic ants, or
COLOSSAL squid?´ I asked hopefully, wobbling
and slipping on the smooth surface of the bath.

His laughter boomed back at me from the
speaker. `Sorry, Ollie,´ he roared. `All I can see
is snow! I made good progress today: I ambled
9.5 kilometres. But then my compass went on
the blink, and it snowed, so I pitched my tent
and stopped for a nice cup of *tea* and a
biscuit.

On Saturday evening, I had to stand on my
head in the bathtub again to get a signal on

the phone. Just as my uncle was giving me his latest update, disaster struck: I overbalanced and crashed over in the bath. My left leg bashed against the cold tap and a jet of **ICY** water poured out. The satellite phone skidded down

towards the plughole, and sat in a puddle that was getting deeper by the second.

I slid around, desperately fumbling with the tap to turn it off. When I picked the phone up, water gushed out of every nook and cranny. I rubbed it dry with a towel, did a headstand, stuck my wet leg out of the window and tried to call again, but it was no use: the phone had drowned.

Nooooooooooooooooooooooooo!

A shudder rattled down my spine. What was I going to do? Even if Uncle Sir Randolph *did* get attacked by Arctic ants, there was nothing I could do about it – I was his **LIFELINE**, and the line had been cut.

I thought about what my uncle does when things go wrong, and I heard his voice in my head say, 'Keep calm, Ollie!'

OK, I thought, taking a deep breath, maybe the satellite phone just needs to dry out properly.

I decided to leave it on the radiator in my bedroom overnight, and try again tomorrow.

The house was like an airport all Sunday: someone arrived as someone else departed, grabbing bags and keys, bustling and hurrying, always complaining about being late.

The twins had got over their costume calamities, and were rehearsing for another ballet show.

Algy had Brain Training Club with the rest of the National Junior Genius Squad.

Dad had a meeting about the new, state-of-the-art penguin house he was designing for Florida Zoo.

Mum was filming a brain operation on Crumbles the Clown for a popular medical reality TV show called *I'm A Celebrity – Cut It Out Of Me!*

I went nowhere fast. I spent a lot of time taking Poochie for walks, or eating raspberry ripple ice cream and reading **Agent Q and the IGLOO DUNGEONS OF DEATH** with Constanza. I checked the satellite phone every half-hour, hoping desperately to get a signal, but it was *still* deader than the dead donkeys in **Agent Q and the DONKEY APOCALYPSE.** I shook it, banged it, pressed every button, but I couldn't even get a crackle, never mind a hiss.

I'd have given up reading comics for a week – no, a month – if I could just hear Uncle Sir Randolph's **BOOMING** voice telling me how much it had snowed today.

WHAT IF . . . something bad had *really* happened to him?

One by one, my family came home in time

for supper. By now I was so worried about my uncle that I decided to come clean about drowning the phone. Before I went downstairs, I tried it one more time. There was a sound like bacon **frying** in a pan, which was an improvement, but I still couldn't get in touch with him.

As we sat around the dining table, I swallowed hard and told everyone what had happened.

'I don't know what to do,' I said finally.

'We must-a do *something*!' cried

Constanza, hurling spaghetti in all directions.

'Keep trying the phone,' answered Mum calmly. 'And if you still haven't been able to make contact in another day or so, we'll open the **CODE RED** envelope. Don't worry, just because your uncle can't talk to us doesn't mean he needs to be rescued.'

'I'm not worried,' said Dad. 'It'll take more than a broken phone to stop Randolph.'

'Do you really think so?' I asked.

'I *know* so.'

I breathed a massive sigh of relief. 'It's as though the expedition's *JINXED,*' I said.

Algy went as red as the toxic tomatoes in *Agent Q and the* **Salad of Doom**.

'Oh no! I forgot to shake the lucky snow

globe!´ he cried. `I've been so busy at university, and with the Junior Genius Squad, and practising for the World Team Chess Championships, and . . .´ He frowned and bit his lip. `Do you think it´s my fault you haven´t heard from Uncle Sir Randolph?´

`Could be,´ I answered, shaking my head. I thought back to Bobby Bragg's **SHOW AND TELL**, when he talked about those evil killer birds called giant petrels. `And **WHAT IF** . . . while the phone's on the blink, he's attacked by psycho seagulls?´

The pictures reeled through my mind. `**WHAT IF** . . . as he tries to escape, the ice cracks, and . . .´

78

My family stared at me, silent and
HORRIFIED, like I'd just done a really noisy
trump.

Poochie's ears drooped, and he gave a
little whine, as though he understood everything
I'd said.

'Oliver!' squealed Emma and Gemma, putting their hands over the dog's ears.

'Nothing *dares* to eat Sir Randolph!' said Constanza.

'But I haven't finished,' I said. `**WHAT IF . . .**'

I laughed at the silly voices I'd given the three killer whales while telling the story. But my family wasn't laughing. They were **FROWNING** like a family of frowners on a frowning holiday to Frownsville, USA.

Uh-oh, I thought, I've done it again. I'm going to get the 'Going Bad Talk'.

(Mum and Dad think I'm going 'like that Peter Cowper next door'. Mum says Peter's a 'difficult teenager' because you can see the top of his underpants over his trousers. Dad thinks he's a **Bad Un** ' because he wears his baseball cap back to front and **grunts** when you say hello to him.)

Peter Cowper

'What I meant was,' I explained quickly, 'Uncle Sir Randolph always gets into tight scrapes on his adventures, but he always survives. "Trouble" is his middle name.'

'No it's not,' said Algy. 'It's Maxwell.'

Even though Mum and Dad said they weren't worried, they kept asking me all evening if I'd managed to get through to my uncle. I kept trying, but all I got was crackles and hisses.

I tried one more time the next morning, but it was hopeless. In the car on the way to school, Constanza frowned at me and muttered in Italian. 'I hope you are wrong in your stories, Oliver,' she said. 'I no like the fibbing with Sir Randolph. *Orribile!*'

'Ignore him, Constanza,' said Emma. 'Oliver's a nerd.'

'But **WHAT IF** . . . someone writes a ballet about Uncle Randolph's Antarctic adventure?' I wondered. '**WHAT IF** . . . in the ballet, he finds the beautiful Snow Princess, CURSED by the wicked Ice Witch to sleep in a frosty tomb until woken by the kiss of a big hairy explorer . . .´

Constanza and the twins smiled and sighed.

`**WHAT IF . . .**´ I continued, `when she wakes, she turns into a vampire penguin, and bites him on the neck?´

ARGHHH!

'You're worse than a nerd,' said Gemma. 'You're a dweeb.'

My little brother didn't say anything. He just sat there, shaking the snow globe over and over again.

'Uncle Sir Randolph will be OK,' I said, light-heartedly. 'Algy's got the snow globe going now.'

But even though Mum and Dad seemed not to be too bothered, I was getting worried.

I bit my lip and stared out of the window.

At school, my project presentation was getting to be worse than the normal PAIN

84

AND TORTURE time. I stood up in front of the
class, and gave them Uncle Sir Randolph's Friday
update, then explained that we were having
`technical difficulties', so there were no more
updates for now.

Peaches did her project update standing in
front of the class in her new emperor-penguin
costume. She looked spectacular, even if one
of the toenails on her wellington-boot feet had
fallen off. She told us about giant penguins that
roamed the Earth millions of years ago but were
now extinct.

`I'm glad they are!' squeaked Millie
Dangerfield.

`Yes, how scary!' agreed Miss Wilkins.

Jamie Ryder showed us a video clip of the
Antarctic night sky he'd downloaded from the

internet. Stars shone through great folds of green wavy light, like a huge fluttering flag.

`These are the Southern Lights,´ he said. `They're just the same as the Northern Lights, but in the south.´

`How beautiful,´ sighed Miss Wilkins.

Toby Hadron said that the Earth is a massive magnet, and a `real´ compass wasn't much use at the South Pole because the needle doesn't know which way to point. He explained why, but I didn't understand a word he said.

`How confusing,´ remarked Miss Wilkins.

Melody Nightingale told us about the **wandering** albatross, a massive seabird with a wingspan of over three metres that lives for fifty years, and spends almost all its life flying.

`How tiring!´ laughed Miss Wilkins.

Melody then gave us a demonstration of the albatross's call. It was like the sound of someone trying very hard to rub marker pen off a white-board, and then **BURPING**.

'It's not fair, Algy,' I complained to my little brother when I got home from school. 'Everyone else is doing fantastic projects, and even though Sir Randolph's *my* uncle, all I've got is a few pins stuck in a map.'

Algy was working out an incredibly complicated maths sum for his university homework, furiously scribbling numbers, lines and shapes in his notebook with one hand, while swirling Uncle Sir Randolph's snow globe with the other.

$$c^2 = a^2 + b^2$$
$$5^2 = 3^2 + b^2$$
$$\frac{3x}{3} = \frac{15}{3}$$

'It's all my fault, Ollie,' he said. 'I'm shaking this all the time now, to try and make his bad luck change.'

As my brother held up the globe to show me, it slipped from his grasp. He grabbed for the lucky charm as it tumbled away from him, plummeting towards the floor.

Nooooooooooooooooooooooooooo!

We both dived, but . . .

We stared in shocked silence at the plastic snowflakes floating in the pool of water, and the family of plastic penguins lying scattered among the fragments of the globe's shattered cover.

'What have I done?' whispered Algy, tears springing to his eyes.

I tried to make my brother feel better. '**WHAT IF . . .** the snow globe is the problem?' I said. '**WHAT IF . . .** it's sending out some kind of anti-radio blocking waves that are interfering with the signal from the satellite phone?'

Algy began clearing up the mess. 'Do you think so?' he sniffed.

'I'll go and try the phone right away,' I replied. 'Don't worry, it'll be all right.'

I hurried down the hallway, but was intercepted by Poochie bursting from the twins' bedroom, with Emma and Gemma in hot pursuit.

The frizzy pepper-grey fur around his head and front legs had been dyed luminous blue, brushed and blown to a soft, feathery fluffiness, and tied with a silver bow. The fur on his back legs had been clipped short and dyed vivid daffodil yellow, and the end of Poochie's tail was now a puffed-up glittery pink pom-pom, shooting up from his bottom like a little hairy firework. To finish off the poor dog's new look, the twins had dressed him in a frilly white tutu.

`Poochie won't play properly,´ grumbled Emma.

`He doesn't like being pampered, and he hates his pom-pom,´ complained Gemma.

`He's a dog,´ I pointed out, watching as Poochie began chasing his tail, spinning round and round in **frantic**, dizzying circles. `He's not a toy.´

`Then *you* look after him,´ said Emma.

`We've got to practise our pas de deux,´ said Gemma.

They **flounced** back into their room and slammed the door. Poochie collapsed at my feet, wagged his tail and stared pleadingly up at me. I picked him up and ruffled his fluffy blue head.

Just then, Dad came up the stairs. He took one look at me, one look at Poochie, shook his head and frowned.

`Oliver,´ he said, and then did his talking-in-capital-letters-thing. `I think We Need To Talk.´

He took me into his office, and told me to sit down next to him at his desk. The drawings for the new penguin house he was designing were spread out in front of us. It looked like three enormous glass igloos, with glass tunnels running under the water to allow the visitors to see the penguins swimming. Inside each igloo were pretend icebergs, and towering snowy-white cliffs. It was spectacular.

Dad dropped *The Deepest Thoughts of the Biggest Brains of All Time* on top of the drawing. It landed with an almighty thump.

The Deepest Thoughts of the Biggest Brains of All Time

`I hope your Thinking´s going well, Oliver,´ he began, nodding at the book.

I stroked my chin, and gazed thoughtfully out of the window. `I've been pondering about the problem of global warming,´ I replied, pausing and nodding like intelligent, deep-thinking people do. `I think . . . it's a problem.´

`Is that it?´ said Dad.

`For now. I need to think about it a bit more.´

Dad sighed. `Oliver, your mum and I are worried about you. We've noticed disturbing signs that you're slipping back into silliness: standing on your head in the bath; trying to frighten Algy and the twins with tall tales –´ he nodded towards Poochie, who was sitting on my lap, trying to bite the big pink pom-pom on the end of his tail – `making this poor dog look like it's survived an explosion in a paint factory . . .´

I began to protest. 'But—'

'And Constanza tells us that you're telling **FIBS** in class again.'

'They're not **FIBS** – they're stories,' I complained. 'And Miss Wilkins doesn't seem to mind. As long as I write them down during playtime detention, she doesn't knock SHINE TIME points off my score any more.'

Dad sighed again. He'd been doing a lot of sighing recently. And frowning.

'Your uncle gave you a very serious job to do, and you don't seem to be taking it very seriously,' he said. 'You're his **LIFELINE**. If things go wrong, you're the one who's supposed to help.'

I nodded. 'Sorry.'

Dad stared at me for a while. 'Don't **Go Bad**, like that Peter Cowper next door. Don't end up grunting, and riding a skateboard all day, showing everyone your underpants, and wearing your hat back to front.´

I was going to say that at least Peter looked happy, but I'm not **Dumb And Brainless;** I knew that wasn't the right answer, so I looked at the floor and shook my head.

`Well, when you sit in your Thinking Room, I want you to think about *that* for a while,´ he said. `I want you to think about being a **Bad Un**.´

He glanced at Poochie. `And I want you to think about giving that poor dog a bath.´

CHAPTER 6

THE ICE PALACE

When I got to school the next morning, all these problems were hanging over me like the bloody blade at the end of **Agent Q and the RETURN OF MADAME GUILLOTINE.**

'What's the matter, Mr Grumpy-boots?' asked Peaches as we filed into class.

I told her everything, including what Dad had said to me.

She reached into her shoulder bag and pulled out a little book called It Could Be Worse: A Tiny Book of Happy Thoughts.

'You need to read this,' she said. 'It has a happy thought for every day of the year. Yesterday's was, "Butterflies are like little angels, sent to fill us full of joy."'

I pulled a face. 'Thanks, Pea. Now I feel sick as well.'

Peaches laughed as she flicked through the pages of the book. 'Today's happy thought is, "Cheer up! At least you're not a bluebottle!"'

Actually, it was Miss Wilkins who made me feel better. She gave me the best news I'd had for ages. The half-term break was coming at the end of the week and, because we had to prepare for a big assembly show on Friday, that morning's presentation would be the last until after the holidays.

'I want you all to get your projects finished over the holidays,' she announced, 'for a final **SHOW AND TELL** the first Monday back at school.'

I sighed with relief. After today, I wouldn't have to suffer this **PAIN AND TORTURE** for a while.

We'd still had no contact with my uncle. Even though he was a **BOLD** adventurer, and 'Trouble' was his middle name, we were all getting really worried about him. When I stood up in front of my class that morning, I was really worried about *me*, because I had absolutely nothing to say.

I thought about what Dad had said.

I thought about being a **Bad Un**.

Then I thought about being laughed at and called names again.

No contest.

I remembered the penguin-house plans spread out on Dad's desk. **WHAT IF . . .** he was *actually* designing an ice palace?

WHAT IF . . . it's the Palace of the Emperor of the Penguins?

`I haven't been able to tell you up to now,´ I said. `But my uncle isn't just Ambling Across the Antarctic. No! He's on a **TOP SECRET** mission to find the mythical Ice Palace of Emperor Penguin Eric III . . .´

Some of the class went, `Ooooooooo!´

`. . . and on Friday night, he phoned to tell

me that his magical wooden compass had found it!'

   To add a bit of magic to my story, I thought about Jamie's presentation on the Southern Lights. **WHAT IF . . .**

   'The palace is only visible when the Southern Lights are switched on,' I told the class.

Peaches's penguin-suit presentation had also given me an idea. **WHAT IF . . .**

`There is an ancient legend,´ I continued, `that in a cave deep in the ice beneath the palace, is the Tomb of the ICE LORD. Inside,

frozen in a massive block of ice, with one frosty foot sticking out, stands the body of . . . Norman the Not Very Nice . . . the most EVIL giant penguin that ever lived.

One vital part of his body is missing: a single colossal Toenail of Doom.´

Bobby Bragg groaned as if he'd got a bad pain somewhere. `Here we go, here we go! Fibbs has got a big fat toe!´ he sang, and a few kids tittered.

I carried on anyway.

`The toenail is kept locked away in another cave on the far side of the palace, and GUARDED day and night. Emperor Eric and his followers will do everything in their POWER to stop the Toenail of Doom from being put back on Norman's foot. It would be a disaster if that ever happened, because the evil giant penguin would defrost, and come back to life. His evil screeches and the flapping of his flippers would cause VIBRATIONS that have the power to freeze the atmosphere. That would start another Ice Age. Within weeks, the world would become one huge snowball!'

`Cool,' said Bobby. `I'd be able to skate all the time!'

`But wouldn't Emperor Eric and the other penguins *want* the Earth to freeze?' asked Toby Hadron.

Oops! I hadn't thought of that! Luckily, Peaches came to my rescue with a really sensible explanation.

`If the seas froze,' she said, `then fish would die, and there wouldn't be anything for the penguins to eat. They'd starve to death.'

Toby opened his mouth to argue, but obviously couldn't think of an answer, so he closed it again. Bobby **glared** at Peaches.

One-nil to the DAB Gang!

`Uncle Sir Randolph trudged up to the penguin palace and hammered on the great ice gates,' I went on. 'They swung open, and two penguin guards faced him, wearing armour and carrying ice spears, shields and swords: they were the legendary Antarctic Ninja Penguins!'

TAKE ME TO YOUR LEADER.

In the icy Throne Room inside the palace, he meets Emperor Eric.

WELCOME, SIR RANDOLPH. WHAT BRINGS YOU HERE?

I HAVE COME TO SEE THE TOMB OF THE ICE LORD.

I WILL TAKE YOU ON ONE CONDITION: TELL ME ABOUT THE TIME YOU HAD YOUR FINGER BITTEN OFF BY A MOUNTAIN LION.

105

'But what Uncle Sir Randolph didn't know was that he'd been followed all the way on his Amble Across the Antarctic,' I told the class. 'Someone else wanted to find the tomb.'

'No!' squealed Millie Dangerfield. 'You don't mean . . .?'

TWO HUGE ICE TROLLS BURST INTO THE THRONE ROOM . . .

THE SAS GANG!

ROOOAR!

THE SHOW-OFF, THE BOFFIN AND THE SPELL QUEEN FOLLOW.

HAND OVER THE TOENAIL OF DOOM AND TAKE US TO NORMAN THE NOT VERY NICE!

NEVER!

Bobby burst out laughing. `Fibbs! Fibbs! You're tickling my ribs!'

`Shush,' hissed Peaches, but he ignored her, and carried on laughing.

`The **SHOW-OFF** said he wanted to freeze the Earth,' I told the class. `Then with evil Norman's help, he'd rule the world, and be able to **SHOW OFF** his amazing ice-skating skills!'

THE SPELL QUEEN'S EYES BEGIN TO GLOW.

HYPNOTIZE HIM!

`The Spell Queen began to chant . . .' I said.

107

`Knuckle, buckle, chuckle, truckle,

SQUidgY, spongy, zombie, bungee,

Punctuation, sanitation,

Devastation, vegetation,

The **SHOW-OFF** is your master now

Hear my **spell**, and take a bow!´

I paused dramatically, staring at the class. `Eric
was spellbound. He bowed like a slave before the
SHOW-OFF . . .´

'The **SHOW-OFF** wouldn't have let your uncle keep his satellite phone,' said Toby Hadron. 'So how come you know all this?'

Luckily, I remembered Melody's project report about the albatross.

'Because he wrote a note on a tea bag and tied it to the leg of a Rocketing Albatross – the fastest bird in the world,' I replied. 'It landed in my garden this morning.'

'Then Sir Randolph's in big trouble!' chuckled Bobby.

CHAPTER 7

COMPASS FAIL!

For once, Bobby was right. Uncle Sir Randolph was actually in more trouble than *Agent Q* was at the end of *Agent Q and the* VOYAGE TO PLANET PERIL when my hero had been knocked unconscious and tied up in a rocket plane that had lost both wings, was on fire, full of deadly tarantulas, plummeting towards the mouth of an erupting volcano and carrying an atomic bomb that was going to go off in nineteen seconds.

Mum and Dad had decided that if we hadn't heard from my uncle by Saturday morning, then we'd put the **CODE RED RESCUE PLAN** in operation, but

$$E = MC^2$$

on Friday night, as Algy was trying to explain **Einstein's Theory of Relativity** to me for about the ten trillionth time, the satellite phone bleeped, and we heard Uncle Sir Randolph's voice.

`Come in, **LIFELINE!** Are you reading me?´

`Come in, **SUPER SNOWMAN,**´ I answered. `Reading you loud and clear. Am I glad to hear you! I thought my phone was broken.´

`Sorry, Ollie, all my fault – I just forgot to change the battery on mine.´

`What's your position and condition?´

`Position: lost. Condition: peckish! I've run

out of Snik-Snaks and I'm down to my last tea bag!' boomed my uncle. `My compass is useless, and I've been ambling round in circles for the last week. I was supposed to be near the South Pole, but haven't a clue where I am now.'

   `Activate the satnav on your phone,' I suggested.

   `I did – it's telling me I'm in Papa Joe's eat-all-you-can bar-b-q blow-out shack in Texas!'

   `What do you want me to do?'

   `HELLLLLLLLLLLLLLLLLLLLLP!'

   `You mean, initiate CODE RED?'

'RED, PURPLE, TANGERINE! I DON'T CARE WHAT COLOUR IT IS, OLLIE! JUST GET ME OUT OF HERE!'

'I won't let you down, **SUPER SNOWMAN**,' I replied. 'Over and out.'

'Yes!' cried Algy happily. 'The snow globe *must* have been the problem! He's safe!'

I stuck out my chest, and held my head high. 'Go and tell Mum and Dad what's happened. I've got to rescue Uncle Sir Randolph.'

My heart was pounding in my chest as I tore open the **CODE RED** envelope and looked at the instructions on the piece of paper inside:

In case of expedition fail, call 999 – NOW!

'Is that it?' I said, checking inside the envelope to see if there were any more **exciting** instructions.

WHAT IF . . . I had to fly out on a special rescue plane, and had to parachute on to the ice with soldiers, snowmobiles and emergency supplies?

But there was nothing.

So I called **999** and explained the problem to the lady who answered.

'We were expecting you to call sooner or later,' she sighed. 'Sir Randolph always gets lost. Don't worry, we know what to do – we've rescued him lots of times before.'

'Oh . . . er, thanks,' I replied. 'Is there anything I can do to help?'

'No, leave it to us.'

I put the phone down and flopped like a LIMP LETTUCE. What a disaster!

Just then, the bedroom door burst open and my entire family charged in. They fired questions at me like machine-gun bullets.

'Is he injured?' demanded Mum.

'Is he safe?' questioned Dad.

'Is he freezing?' worried Emma.

'Is he starving?' wondered Gemma.

'Is he going to die?' yowled Constanza.

'Is he *really* in Texas?' asked Algy.

I told them not to worry, and that help was on its way.

Luckily, it was half-term, so I didn't have to admit that my uncle's Antarctic Amble was **abandoned.** We soon got a message that he'd been found, and taken off the ice. Then we heard that he was well, and was being flown home straight away for medical checks.

On Sunday night, an ambulance pulled up outside our house, and Dad pushed Uncle Sir Randolph down the garden path and into the house in a wheelchair. The explorer's face was red and raw, and his wild hair had gone completely grey and fizzed around his head like SMOKE from a bushfire.

My uncle's little dog scampered down the hall and launched himself into his arms, licking his face gleefully.

`Poochie!' he boomed. `You've had a haircut! It suits you! What a good thing you didn't come with me. When I ran out of Snik-Snaks, I'd have been forced to eat *you*!'

The twins **gasped**.

'You'll do anything when it's a matter of LIFE or DEATH,' he said. 'Once, in the Australian Outback, I was so hungry I had to slice lumps off my leg and eat them.'

'Eeuwww!' squealed Emma.

'Gross!' sqeaked Gemma.

'I'll show you the scars when I'm back on my feet!' said Uncle Sir Randolph, and roared with laughter.

'Ollie!' he bellowed when he saw me. 'My hero!'

'I only made a phone call,' I protested.

'But that was your job, and you did it well.'

I smiled weakly. I was more doomed than Donald Doomed, of 13 Doomed Street, Doomedtown, Doomedshire, Doomedland. What

118

was I going to report on back at school? That Uncle Sir Randolph had got lost? That he couldn't go on because he'd run out of Snik-Snaks? That he'd had to be rescued? That he'd *FAILED*?

I couldn't sleep with wondering what to do. I tried reading **Agent Q and the** Killer Cat Catastrophe, but kept reading the same part of the story over and over again.

*

While we drove to school on Monday after half-term, I stared out of the window, saying nothing as the twins kept up a stream of ballet babble, and Algy sat with his fingers in his ears reading a book on advanced algebra. Constanza hummed a happy Italian tune as she **HONKED** the horn at other drivers.

`Is good that Sir Randolph returns in the house, eh, Ollie?´ she said.

`Yeah, great.´

She sighed. `*Eroico!*´

As I stood in front of the class to give my update, I saw Bobby Bragg grinning like one of the vile little goblins in *Agent Q and the* Secret Cities of the Underworld.

I can't do it, I thought. I can't say

what really happened. I have to keep my uncle's **failure** a secret.

I took a deep breath and said, 'Do you remember before the holiday, I got a message from Uncle Sir Randolph, attached to the leg of a Rocketing Albatross?'

HELP, DABMAN!
CAPTURED BY
SHOW-OFF!
FIND ICE PALACE
BY SOUTHERN LIGHTS.
SIR RANDOLPH
P.S. PLEASE BRING
SOME MORE
TEA BAGS.

THIS IS A JOB FOR...

Defenders of Planet Earth Security!

'Never fear!' laughed Bobby Bragg. 'The D.O.P.E.S. are here!'

I carried on. 'My snow globe teleporter was broken,' I said. 'So Captain Sensible and I needed another way to get to the Antarctic . . .'

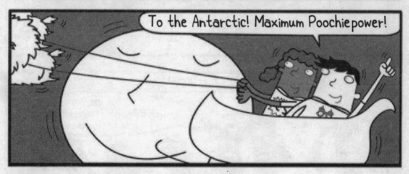

'In seconds we were over the ice,' I told the class. 'The Southern Lights lit up the sky, and we saw it: the Ice Palace of Emperor Eric III, glinting in the snow below us. But it was heavily guarded by ice trolls. How could we get inside? Captain Common Sense rummaged in her utility bag and came up with a plan . . .'

`The penguins told me that Uncle Sir Randolph was being held captive in the palace,´ I said. `And that the **SHOW-OFF** and his **DASTARDLY** gang were about to wake Norman the Not Very Nice!´

`Save him, *DABMAN*,´ squeaked Millie Dangerfield. `Save us all!´

Miss Wilkins sighed. `I was hoping that today you´d give us a more regular update on your uncle´s expedition,´ she said. `But I *am* curious to know what happened next. Go on, Oliver.´

`Well, miss,´ I continued. `We **waddled** through the ice palace in our penguin costumes and found the Boffin´s secret **REFRIGERATED** science lab. Inside, we found rows of huge test tubes containing half-formed ice trolls.´

'Just then, we heard the squawking of hundreds of penguins coming from a room just down the corridor, followed by a familiar voice . . .'

`The world is in terrible **DANGER**!' I said to
the class. `If the **SHOW-OFF** joins the Toenail of
Doom to Norman the Not Very Nice's foot, we're
in big trouble!'

'Then what are you doing here talking to us?' said Bobby. 'Why aren't you in the Antarctic saving the world?'

The others muttered and nodded.

Bobby had *really* got me this time! The class stared at me, waiting for my answer. Excuses whirled around in my mind like snowflakes in a **BLIZZARD**, melting away before I could catch them.

'Er . . . I . . . er . . .'

Bobby smirked, enjoying his moment of victory.

'It's **OBVIOUS** why he's here,' said Peaches, rummaging in her bag.

'Is it? I mean, it is!' I said. 'Er . . . tell them, Pea!'

My best friend held up something small,

shiny and silver. `**DAB**MAN was in such a rush to get to the Antarctic that he forgot this,´ she said. `The XT47 *Sub-ionic* Toenail Clipper!´

I felt my jaw drop. The class gaped like goldfishes. I thought Miss Wilkins's eyes would pop out of her head.

`If the **SHOW-OFF** succeeds in his evil plan, then this is the only thing that will cut the Toenail of Doom off Norman the Not Very Nice's foot,´ explained Peaches, making her way to the front of the class and handing me the clippers.

`Pea, you told **FIBS**!´ I whispered.

`They're not **FIBS** – they're stories,´ she whispered back, winking at me.

I held the clippers high over my head. `*Now* I can save the world!´

129

'Finish your project first,' said Miss Wilkins.

'*Then* you can save the world.'

CHAPTER 8

TOES

At lunchtime, I asked Peaches to sit at a table in the corner, so we wouldn't be disturbed.

`Pea, I've got something to tell you, but it's **TOP SECRET!**' I said, glancing around to make sure no one could hear me. `Uncle Sir Randolph isn't Ambling Around the Antarctic any more. He got lost and had to be rescued. He's at my house right now.'

Peaches gasped. `Ollie, you've got to tell the

truth to the class!'

'I can't! Bobby will rip me to shreds.'

Peaches frowned and nodded. 'Don't worry, we'll work something out.' Her face brightened. 'Can I meet him?' she asked. 'I've never met a real explorer before.'

'Why don't you come round for tea after school?'

Peaches arranged it with her mum as we waited for Constanza to pick me up. Our nanny was sixteen minutes late, and *dashed* into school, waving her arms above her head as if she was batting away a swarm of invisible flies.

'Sorry, Oliver!' she cried. 'I get your sisters from the ballet academy and – boom! bang! boom! – the car breaks up!'

`The car broke *down*,´ I corrected, hurrying her out of school before she could talk to Miss Wilkins and let the cat out of the bag about Uncle Sir Randolph.

Constanza shrugged. `Up, down, it no work.´

`Peaches is coming home with us for tea,´ I told her.

Our nanny beamed, and planted a noisy kiss on each of Peaches's cheeks. `*Ciao, bella!*´

Emma and Gemma sat in the back of the car looking like the Princesses Grump and Grouchy from the land of BADTEMPER.

`Hurry up!´ cried Emma. `Constanza's made us late for Madame Sylvie's stage make-up workshop!´

`And now *you're* making us even later,´ yelled Gemma. `We're being turned into VAMPIRES tonight.´

The picture flashed into my brain. `**WHAT IF** . . . Madame Sylvie is actually a **VAMPIRE**? **WHAT IF** . . . she uses magic undead paint that turns you into **VAMPIRES** too?´

Algy laughed. `Too late! These two are blood-suckers already!´

Peaches and I climbed into the back seats as the terrible twosome attacked my giggling little brother.

`Help, Ollie,´ he cried. `Get the garlic!´

`Hi, Peaches,´ chorused my sisters when they saw my best friend.

`What's your favourite ballet?´ asked Emma, leaning over her seat. `Isn't *Romeo and Juliet* simply divine?´

`Don't you think *Swan Lake* is just wonderful?´ gushed Gemma.

`I don't like ballet,´ replied Peaches.

The twins gasped, gazed at my friend in astonishment, then turned round and ignored her for the rest of the trip home.

`Great news, children!´ said Dad when we walked through the front door. `Uncle Randolph will be staying with us for a few more weeks.´

`Even better news, kids,´ boomed my uncle, pointing at his bandaged foot. `I've got frostbite! I'm having two toes **CUT OFF** tomorrow!'

`Awesome!' cried Algy, and Sir Randolph's barrelling laughter filled the house once more, as Poochie yipped and yapped around his feet.

I introduced Peaches to him.

`Is she your girlfriend?' he chortled, digging me hard in the ribs and giving me a huge wink. `A man needs a good woman by his side.'

`No,' I said quickly, feeling my face go hot. `She's my best friend.'

`Do you have a good woman by *your* side, Sir Randolph?' asked Peaches.

The twins gaped at her. Mum frowned and

gave a small, sharp hiss as if she was in pain. Poochie stopped barking and lay down with his head on his paws, glancing up at his master. A tense, **DEATHLY** quiet filled the room.

Peaches glanced around anxiously. `Did I say something wrong?´ she asked.

My uncle seemed to shrink like a deflating balloon, bowing his head and staring at his hands. `Bunty,´ he whispered. My dad squeezed his brother's shoulder.

Uncle Sir Randolph looked up at Peaches, his intense grey eyes softened by tears. `Life's

never been the same since my beloved Bunty was carried off into the rainforest by a troop of orang-utans, never to be seen again. I searched and searched, but . . . she's gone forever.'

`*Tragico!*' sobbed Constanza.

`It was my fault,' he said, his voice quivering. `Bunty always wanted to come with me on my expeditions, but I wouldn't allow it. This time she insisted, and I said yes. Then it all went HORRIBLY WRONG . . .'

A single tear rolled down his cheek, and he swiped it away angrily.

`What a beautiful ballet it would make,' sighed Emma.

Gemma nodded. `Like *Romeo and Juliet* . . . but with monkeys.'

'I'm sorry,' said Peaches quietly. 'I didn't know . . .'

No one spoke for a moment. Then Algy broke the silence. 'Uncle Sir Randolph, tell Peaches the story of when you were attacked by the flock of **man-eating** ducks on Lake Titicaca.'

A wide, **BRILLIANT** smile lit up my uncle's ruddy face. 'I'd be delighted, young Algy!' he replied, slapping my brother hard on the shoulder, almost knocking him into the kitchen.

Everyone smiled with relief, and marched into the living room to hear the tale of heroism and **DANGER**, leaving me and Peaches standing in the hall.

'He's super,' she said.

'Yeah,' I muttered. 'And special.'

`What's the matter?´

`I wish I'd never told Miss Wilkins that he was my uncle,´ I replied, pushing my hands into my pockets and staring at my feet. `I wanted everyone to think *I* was Super And Special, because *he* was an explorer, and a hero. But he failed, Pea. Now I think about it, Uncle Sir Randolph *always* fails. He's a RUBBISH explorer.´

`Ollie! That's a terrible thing to say!´

I blushed, and sighed. `I know. I'm sorry. It's just that . . . I'm **DOOMED** when we get back to school.´

`Oh, poor you,´ snapped Peaches. `At least your girlfriend's not been **kidnapped** by orang-utans, and you're not going to have two toes **CHOPPED OFF** tomorrow!´ She stomped off down the hall towards the living room. `I want to

142

hear about the **man-eating** ducks of Lake Titicaca, even if you don't.'

Uncle Sir Randolph was back on form, telling his tales, and filling the house with laughter once more, so I pumped him for interesting information about his expedition that I could use in my project presentation.

'Did you have to WRESTLE any wild animals?' I asked. 'Like . . .'

'Not this time, Oliver,' he admitted. 'The worst thing that happened was when a seagull **pooped** on my head.'

'Well . . . did you see the Southern Lights?'

'No, I didn't. Someone must have turned off the lights before I got there!' He chuckled.

'Well . . . did you get lost in a blizzard,' I tried, 'and have to pitch your tent in hundred-mile-an-hour winds, which buried you under ten metres of snow, so that you had to dig your way to safety with the spoon you use to stir your *tea*?'

`No, I got lost because my compass broke, and the weather wasn't too bad, actually.´ He grinned. `The most terrible thing that happened was when I ran out of *tea* bags, and had to suck on the old ones!´

As everyone laughed along with my uncle, I tried to imagine saying that to my class when I gave them my next update. It wasn't hard to imagine the very different kind of laughter I'd get from *them*: they'd be laughing *at* me, not *with* me.

Uncle Sir Randolph went into hospital the next day, and had his operation.

`Look at these!´ he **BOOMED**, when Mum and Dad wheeled him back through the front door. He held up a glass container with what looked like two BLACK SLUGS swimming in a pale, yellowy liquid. `The surgeon gave me my toes as a souvenir! I can put them on top of my TV at home, next to the finger the mountain lion bit off, and the teeth that gorilla knocked out when I was rambling in the rainforests! If I carry on like this, I'll end up living in pieces on a shelf!'

`Did you do the operation, Mum?' asked my brother.

'I do brains, Algy,' she replied. 'Not toes.'

Uncle Sir Randolph got out of the wheelchair and staggered into the living room on crutches.

'You are so brave, Signore Randolph,' said Constanza.

'You're like Dimetri Babkin,' said Emma. 'Who danced *Snow White* with a sprained ankle.'

'Or Anna Globa,' said Gemma, 'who danced *Sleeping Beauty* with a broken fingernail.'

Uncle Sir Randolph laughed. 'I'm a dopey explorer who should have put on an extra pair of socks!'

I stood by the door and watched my Super And Special family fussing over my heroic uncle. I felt bad about it, but I couldn't join in. So I slouched off up the stairs to my Thinking Room.

There was no doubt about it: when I got to school, I was in even deeper trouble than *Agent Q* in *Agent Q and the* Mines of Mystery, when he was nine kilometres underground, at the bottom of a lake teeming with man-eating fish, shackled with chains, tied up in a bag, and locked in a steel box, next to a poisonous gas canister that was about to burst in twenty-three seconds!

CHAPTER 9

RUMBLED

In the morning, Peaches was waiting for me at the school gates.

'Ollie, be SENSIBLE: you've got to tell the truth,' she said. 'You'll only get found out if you don't.'

'OK, Pea,' I replied. 'But it's going to be as **Dull And Boring** as the World **Dull And Boring** Championships, in Dull, the capital of Boringland.'

151

'Having two toes chopped off is really interesting,' she said.

'Yeah, but sucking on a cold *tea* bag isn't!'

When I saw all the amazingly Dynamic And **BRILLIANT** things everyone else had done with their projects, my heart sank.

Bobby Bragg had made a model of an iceberg, floating in a tank of water, to show how only one-ninth of the berg shows above the water. He said that they were often full of caves and cracks, and the ice in them was sometimes blue because it was so thick. Then, to

show how **DANGEROUS** icebergs were, he sank a model of the *Titanic*.

Toby Hadron showed models he'd made of all the different kinds of snowflake there are, and said that no two flakes are the same.

Jamie Ryder told the heroic story of Captain Scott, whose team just failed to win the race to be the first to reach the South Pole. Sadly, they **FROZE** to death on the journey home, just eleven miles short of their camp.

At least Captain Scott failed heroically, I thought. How could I admit that my uncle had just . . . *failed*?

My heart thumped as I shuffled to the front of the class. My throat was tight, and my mouth felt as parched as the land **Agent Q**'s spy plane crashes in at the start of **Agent Q**

and the DESERT OF NO RETURN. Peaches nodded and smiled sympathetically.

`Erm . . . I've got something to tell you all,´ I began. `Uncle Sir Randolph . . .´

Bobby Bragg grinned at me. I licked my dry lips, and coughed nervously.

`Uncle Sir Randolph . . .´ I took a deep breath. `. . . was trapped in an ice-dungeon in the Palace of Eric III, Emperor of the Penguins, and D.O.P.E.S. had gone to the rescue, disguised as penguins.´

Bobby Bragg **moaned** loudly. `Not again!´ he cried.

`Just as Captain Common Sense and I set off to find the dungeon,´ I continued, `we came face to face with one of the Boffin's vicious ice trolls . . .´

I thought about what Bobby had said in his presentation about icebergs. 'When we came round, we were inside a gloomy, **glistening** cave,' I continued. 'The walls curved and twisted in great folds of blue and white ice, and shone with a cold, eerie blue light. Huge, sharp **ICICLES** hung from the roof, as if the cave had teeth. It was like being in the mouth of a horrible ice monster. Standing in the centre, on a gleaming pedestal, and encased in a crust of glittering frost, lay the frozen body of Norman the Not Very Nice.'

155

`The block of ice wrapped around the giant penguin began to crack,´ I said. `Huge chunks tumbled down and shattered on the floor of the cave. Everyone ducked for cover as splinters like carving knives sliced through the air.

`Norman the Not Very Nice flapped his icy wings, and wiggled his icy toes. The cruel, curving beak cracked open and Norman threw back his head and let rip with a deafening screech.

`The sound shook the palace, and carried out into the FREEZING wastes of Antarctica. The ground began to shake.´

SKREEAWWWWWK-
HAKKA-
HAKKA-

SKREEEEEEK!

`What was happening, Ollie?´ asked Millie Dangerfield.

`It was the start of another Ice Age,´ I replied. `The ice had already started to grow! Soon the temperature would plunge even lower than the record minus ninety-eight degrees Celsius!´

THE SAS GANG THROW DABMAN AND CAPTAIN COMMON SENSE IN THE DUNGEON

WITHOUT THESE YOU ARE POWERLESS!

AT LAST! WE WIN!

DON'T CATCH COLD!

HA-HA-HAAAAA!

CALL THIS A RESCUE? I HOPE YOU'VE GOT A PLAN.

ER, NO. THIS WASN'T SUPPOSED TO HAPPEN.

Pants on fire! We're in a frosty pickle!

I paused in my story. Uh-oh. How was I going to get them out of this mess when they didn't have their gadgets to help them?

'Go on, Ollie,' said Millie Dangerfield. 'How did **DABMAN** escape?'

'He didn't escape,' sneered Bobby Bragg. 'Sir Randolph isn't in the Antarctic any more. He's been staying at the Fibbs' house since last Sunday!'

The class gasped.

Bobby stood up and pointed at me. 'He's telling big fat **FIBS** again! Sir Randolph got lost, walked around in circles for a few days then had to be rescued. My dad saw it in the brief news section on page thirty-four of the *Daily Comet* yesterday.' He waved a newspaper cutting triumphantly in the air, then gave it to Miss Wilkins.

My teacher looked shocked as she read. `Oliver, is this true?´

My tummy twisted. My heart pounded. My shoulders slumped. `Yes, miss.´ I stared at the ground. I opened my mouth to say more, but couldn´t find any words to explain.

`And you didn´t think to tell us?´

I shook my head.

`Ten SHINE TIME points off your score, Oliver Tibbs,´ she growled. (Down to minus five.) `And TWO playtime detentions.´

When I sat down, Peaches growled at me like the bulldog with a toothache in *Agent Q and the* HOUNDS OF HELLFIRE.

`I told you,´ she hissed.

At morning and afternoon break, I had to stay in and write out my fib, and when Constanza came to pick me up, she and Miss Wilkins had one of their whispered chats. I caught words like, `shocking!´, `disgraceful!´, `shame!´ and `toad-in-the-hole´.

`*Cattivo!*´ cried Constanza as I got into the car.

`I´m not a naughty boy,´ I said. `I´m just . . . *stupido*.´

Algy and the twins were already in the car, and when they heard what I´d done they gasped.

`You´re in trouble,´ said Emma.

`You´re in *serious* trouble,´ said Gemma.

`You´ll get grounded,´ said Algy.

They were totally right. That evening, my

entire family gathered around to interrogate
me.

'Why, Oliver, why?' demanded Dad.

'I was too embarrassed to tell the truth,'
I admitted. 'I didn't want to tell the class that
Uncle Sir Randolph was a FAILURE.'

Everyone began to yell and wave their arms
about like the maniac meerkats in *Agent Q
and the* CRAZY ZOO.

'LEAVE THE LAD ALONE!' bellowed Uncle Sir
Randolph. There was so much yelling going on
that no one had noticed him enter the room.
'I WANT TO SPEAK TO OLIVER IN PRIVATE!'

They all scuttled out, including Poochie.
My uncle closed the door behind them, hobbled
over to a chair and sat down heavily. After
all the shouting and screaming, the room

was **SPOOKILY** quiet. The old clock on the mantelpiece ticked and tocked gently. Uncle Sir Randolph stared at me for ages, saying nothing, and soon the stillness in the room seemed even louder than the yelling.

I looked down, tracing the pattern on the carpet with the toe of my shoe. My heart raced. I could feel my uncle's **fierce** grey eyes boring into me. I'd never known him to be so quiet before; it was seriously scary. I'd been in **Big Trouble** because of my Big *FIBS* in the past, but this time I was in *Mega* Trouble.

At last, Uncle Sir Randolph took a deep breath, and exhaled slowly. `I want to know exactly what you told your classmates about my Antarctic Amble.´

I told him how everybody had found my daily reports **Dull And Boring**: `You walked a bit; it snowed a bit; you had a cup of *tea*. They were laughing at me . . . at *you*! I *had* to make the updates more interesting, so I added some Arctic ants, a giant squid, and a few ninja penguins . . .´

As I told Uncle Sir Randolph my *DABMAN* story, he stared intently at me. I got to the part in the fib about being locked up in the **FREEZING**

dungeon without our gadgets, and said, `That's
as far as I'd got when Bobby Bragg told everyone
you'd failed . . . I mean, been rescued.´

That **horrible** loud quietness crept into
the room again as my uncle sat and stared at
me some more.

`You're right, Ollie,´ he said softly. `I *am* a
failure. I'm a useless explorer.´

`No, you're not! You found the lost pyramid of King Tutti-frutti, and the lair of the legendary Not Yeti, and the buried treasure of Captain Bluenose, and the secret gold mine of Grumpy Gordon McGrundy, and the Magical Dancing Clogs of the ancient Queen of Cleves,´ I said. `You've fought bandits, and mountain lions, and **MAN-EATING** ducks!´

`I made it all up,´ Uncle Sir Randolph replied. `But the SCAR on your forehead . . .´

`I got that cleaning the toilet at home: the lid fell on my head.´

`And your missing finger . . .´

`I was careless chopping a cucumber.´

You could have bowled me over with a **burp**. `But . . . but . . . but . . .´

`Imagine what it´s like growing up with a **BRILLIANT**, prize-winning little brother,´ he said.

`But I *can* imagine it!´

`And then he married a **BRILLIANT** brain surgeon,´ continued my uncle. `And had **BRILLIANT** children: two super ballerinas, a maths genius, and you, Oliver – a great thinker. I can´t compete with all that. I´m useless at everything, so I **ESCAPE** and go wandering about in different parts of the world. But, even then, something always goes wrong!´

`So, when you come back, you tell *FIBS*,´ I said.

Uncle Sir Randolph nodded. `Big fat ones.´

I dragged a chair over and sat down in front of him. `So do I! I'm not a great thinker – I only go into my Thinking Room to read *Agent Q* comics.´

Uncle Sir Randolph's mouth dropped open in amazement. `You mean, you're **Dull And Boring** too?´

I grinned and nodded. `I'm **BRILLIANT** at being **Dull And Boring**.´

He roared with laughter and slapped me hard on my arm, knocking me off my chair. `I always take a few *Agent Q* comics with me to read on my expeditions. They're the inspiration for my tall tales.´

`Of course!´ I said, rubbing my arm and

getting up from the carpet. `**Q** gets kidnapped by bandits in *Agent Q and the* INVASION OF THE SPHINX MEN. And he's attacked by a vicious mountain goat in *Agent Q and the* **Goat Ghouls of Kathmandu.** And he nearly gets eaten by killer cockatoos in *Agent Q and the* Bird Lady of Aldershot.´

`All my best ***FIBS*** are "borrowed" from those comics,´ admitted my uncle.

`Maybe we're both "Going Bad" like that Peter Cowper next door,´ I said.

`And maybe it's time we both stopped telling big fat ***FIBS*** and started telling the truth.´ He looked me in the eye. `Starting with my talk at your school next week.´

CHAPTER 10

THE TRUTH – HONEST!

On the morning of the talk, I begged and pleaded with my uncle not to do it, but he was determined to be honest. `The **FIBS** have got to stop, Ollie,´ he said.

He arrived at school in style, balancing on my old skateboard and being pulled along by Poochie to take the pressure off his injured

foot. The hall was packed and BUZZING, as every pupil and teacher crowded in to hear my uncle tell them of his Antarctic adventure.

Our headmistress, Mrs Broadside, stood up to introduce him.

`We are the luckiest school in the country!´ she began. `Today we have a real hero in our midst. The world-famous, dashing and brave explorer, Sir Randolph Maxwell Templeton Tibbs, has come to talk to us about his thrilling, death-defying, single-handed Amble Across the Antarctic.´

Everyone clapped and cheered as Uncle Sir Randolph stood up. Poochie was tired out, and curled up asleep on the skateboard next to him. Bobby Bragg whispered something to Toby and Hattie, and they all sniggered.

`Good morning, children and teachers,´ my uncle began. `Thank you for asking me to come today and talk about my trip. I´ve been looking at the projects Year Six have done, and I have to say, they are all splendid!´

He showed his first slide. `The main thing I discovered about the Antarctic is that it´s a very snowy place. In fact, to be honest, it was far too snowy for me.´

Bobby gave a short snort of laughter, and I

saw Mrs Broadside turn round and glare in
his direction.

My uncle pointed at the photograph filling
the screen. 'I took this photo on day one, when
I ambled thirteen kilometres. As you can see,
it snowed.

'I took this
photo on day
two, when I
ambled nine
and a half
kilometres. It
snowed about the
same amount as on day one.

'I took this photo on
day three, when I ambled
five kilometres. It snowed

all day, and probably a bit heavier than on
day two.

    `I took this photo
on the morning of day
four . . .

    `But it
stopped snowing in
the afternoon, and so I

    took this photo.
I ambled seven and
a quarter kilometres
that day.´

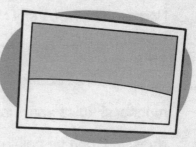

    Bobby Bragg smirked at me, and
nudged Toby Hadron, sitting next to him.
`Sir,´ he called out. `What we want to know is,

did you find the Tomb of the Ice Lord?'

Panic zinged through my body like a **zillion volts** of electricity. My face burned, as a ripple of titters and giggles spread along the line of kids from my class.

Uncle Sir Randolph coughed, and shuffled his feet. `I . . . er . . .'

Bobby grinned. `And were you really attacked by Arctic ants? And did you defeat Norman the Not Very Nice?'

`That's enough shouting out, Bobby Bragg!' snapped Mrs Broadside. `Remember your manners! Raise your hand if you want to ask a question, and be polite to our guest.'

Millie Dangerfield put her hand up shyly, her face a mask of worry. `Sir, are we going to get another ice age?' she asked quietly.

Uncle Sir Randolph stood in silence for a moment, scanning the sea of faces staring back at him. I scrunched my body into a ball, and held my head in my hands as I waited for him to tell the truth and seal my doom.

`Of course I found the Tomb of the Ice Lord!' he **ROARED** at Bobby Bragg. `Of course I was attacked by Arctic ants! I thought Oliver had given you my reports . . . or weren't you listening?'

Bobby glanced around nervously, and his mouth opened and closed a few times.

`I'll tell you what happened,' boomed Uncle Sir Randolph. `I was locked in an icy dungeon with **DAB**MAN and Captain Common Sense. The Show-off had made a big mistake, because underneath the penguin suit **DAB**MAN was wearing his special **Pants on Fire.** He quickly put them into action . . .´

I couldn't believe it: Uncle Sir Randolph was telling the rest of *my* story, and adding a few **FIBS** of his own!

'**DAB**MAN and Captain Common Sense swung into action,' he continued.

THE SOUTHERN LIGHTS SPELL OUT A MESSAGE TO THE PENGUINS . . .

THE SHOW-OFF HAS TRICKED YOU! WHEN THE SEA FREEZES, ALL THE FISH WILL DIE AND YOU WILL STARVE!

'They were so enraged with being tricked that the air was filled with the angry squawks of thousands of angry penguins as they stormed the palace,' continued Uncle Sir Randolph. 'But in the meantime the three of us were under attack by an army of ice trolls.'

'It looked like we were doomed,' said Uncle Sir Randolph, 'but as the ice trolls closed in for the kill, dozens of ninja penguins charged towards them, screaming ear-splitting, high-pitched squawks. The pain was terrible, and we fell to the ground, covering our ears. But the trolls exploded into a million shards of glittering ice, shattered by the intense cries of the penguins.´

Uncle Sir Randolph paused. Everyone was gripped by his story. The room was so quiet that I could hear Millie Dangerfield's knees knocking.

Then a look of panic crept into my uncle's eyes. I knew that look: he couldn't think what to say next. He'd dried up! I jumped to my feet.

`Captain Common Sense and **DABMAN** dashed to the Throne Room,´ I said, making everyone turn and stare at me. `The **SAS GANG**

and Norman the Not Very Nice were celebrating
their victory with fish-flavoured ice-lollies.´

`Meanwhile, Captain Common Sense had
crept up behind Norman,´ I said. `She pulled the

XT47 **Sub-ionic** Toenail Clipper from her sensible bag, and . . . SNIP! . . . she chopped the Toenail of Doom from Norman's foot.

'When the Spell Queen fainted, Emperor Eric became instantly un-hypnotized. He and the other penguins put Norman the Not Very Nice back in the Tomb of the Ice Lord,' I said. 'Captain Common Sense very sensibly chopped the Toenail of Doom into hundreds of tiny pieces. Then the ninja penguins set out on a march around Antarctica, spreading the clippings far and wide across the ice, to be buried forever beneath the snow.'

'And once again,' roared Uncle Sir Randolph, 'the two D.O.P.E.S. had saved the Earth from disaster!'

'Hurray!' cheered Millie Dangerfield.

Bobby Bragg grumbled under his breath, '*FIBS* and lies will pop your eyes!'

Uncle Sir Randolph heard him. 'So you think

we made it up, do you?' he asked, pulling off his shoe and sock. `Then take a look at this!'

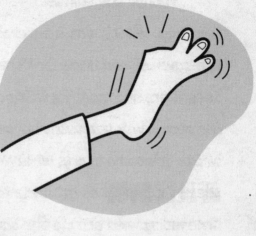

The kids gasped as he held up his foot for all to see.

`And here are the toes the ice troll sliced off!'

The hall echoed to sound of about 250 people going, `Eughhhhhhhh!'

Hattie Hurley was sick all over Bobby Bragg . . .

185

. . . then she fainted.

Miss Wilkins was a bit cross about this. She gave me and Uncle Sir Randolph a playtime detention, and made us write down the rest of our story. What *actually* happened was that I wrote down the story, while Miss Wilkins listened **SPELLBOUND** as my uncle told her about the time he crawled around the caves of Catalonia, and stumbled into the lair of a venomous Spanish squish-squash snake.

`Was that a *FIB* too?´ I asked him when the playtime bell rang, and our detention was over.

`More of an exaggeration,´ he whispered. `I took a nap in one of the caves, and woke up with a worm on my nose.´

My classmates came in from the playground, and Uncle Sir Randolph said his goodbyes. Then, as we waved and cheered, he stepped on to my old skateboard, and shouted, 'Mush!' Poochie gave a few happy barks, and they trundled off down the road.

Peaches nudged me, and whispered, 'Do you think he'll get lost on his way home?'

I took the satellite phone from Peaches's special holster that dangled at my hip. 'I've got this,' I grinned. 'Just in case.'

I spent the rest of the day being high-fived by just about every kid in school. There was a real buzz about the place. Only Bobby Bragg and Hattie Hurley weren't happy. Bobby had to wear his PE kit for the rest of the day, because his ordinary clothes were covered in Hurley hurl.

It was *definitely* a Memorable Day!

CHAPTER 11

GROUNDED

When I got home from school, Mum, Dad and Uncle Sir Randolph were sitting in the living room looking like they'd caught a bad case of **Grim and Grumpy-itis.** Even Poochie was glum and silent at my uncle's feet.

`Sit down, Oliver,´ ordered Dad. `You and Sir Randolph are in **Big Trouble.**´

`Why?´

`**FIBS,**´ answered Mum.

`I told your parents everything, Ollie,´ said my uncle. `Not just about our *FIB* at school, but how I've made up *all* my perilous adventures.´

Constanza, Algy and the twins gasped, obviously as shocked at this news as I had been.

`It's true,´ he said, nodding sadly, `and I'm sorry.´

`Will the curse of Black Jack Tibbs always bring shame on us?´ said Dad.

(Black Jack was the black sheep of our family. He was a rogue and a rascal, and the first Tibbs ever to `**Go Bad**´, over 200 years ago.)

`You are both grounded for a week,´ said Mum.

'But, Charlotte,' complained Uncle Sir Randolph, 'they're not really *FIBS* – they're more like . . . stories.'

It was no use: that was *my* excuse, and it never worked.

Constanza tutted and wagged her finger at my uncle. '*Cattivo!*' she said, smiling. 'You are the naughty boy like Oliver, and naughty boys must have the ice cream, yes?'

So every evening, as my **BRILLIANT** family went here, there and everywhere doing their **BRILLIANT** things, Constanza, Uncle Sir Randolph and I stayed at home, sitting on the sofa, eating raspberry ripple ice cream, and reading **Agent Q** comics.

On Saturday, everyone stayed in to watch a TV programme about Dad's new penguin house at Florida Zoo. It was amazing: an ice palace fit for an emperor penguin.

When it finished, we began to chat **excitedly** about the programme. Uncle Sir Randolph was just saying that yet another architecture award would be winging its way to Dad when he suddenly leaped to his foot, hopping around and crying, 'Bunty! Bunty!'

Poochie joined him, doing little jumps and **yapping** noisily.

The news had come on after Dad's zoo programme, and luckily we hadn't turned the TV off.

`Breaking news,´ said the newsreader. `A woman has been discovered living WILD, high in the rainforest mountains of Borneo. She was found by cameramen filming a documentary about orang-utans for the BBC.´

The famous nature presenter David Rabbitburrow came on screen. `The woman just wandered into our camp one morning,´ he said. `She seemed to be looking for someone, and the only word she would say was "Randolph".

`It is believed that the WILD WOMAN OF BORNEO, as she is now called, could possibly be Bunty Templeton Tibbs, wife of the famous explorer Sir Randolph Templeton Tibbs. She was carried off many years ago by a troupe of orang-utans, and has never been seen since.´

`That's my Bunty!´ cried our uncle.

'She needs a haircut,' whispered Emma.

'She needs a bath,' added Gemma.

'When you told me *all* your stories were **FIBS**, I thought *that* was a **FIB** too,' I said to my uncle.

'No! That one was true!' He laughed, his grey eyes shining with joy. 'And it's going to have a happy ending!' He hobbled towards the living-room door. 'I'm going to amble to the airport, fly to the Far East and bring back my Bunty.'

'*Romantico!*' said Constanza.

'But you can't go to Borneo,' said Algy. 'You're grounded.'

Mum laughed. 'I think under the circumstances, Algy, we'll forgive Uncle Sir Randolph for telling **FIBS**, and let him fetch Aunt Bunty home.'

While my uncle packed his rucksack, my dad made a few phone calls, and in no time at all they were climbing into the car and racing away to the airport.

On Monday morning, I stood up in front of my classmates and told them the story of Uncle Sir Randolph and Bunty.

`How incredible!' said Miss Wilkins.

`She was kidnapped by orangu-tans?' sneered Bobby Bragg. `Tibbs, Tibbs, you're telling more fibs!'

I couldn't help feeling a small thrill of triumph as I pressed a key on Miss Wilkins's computer, and an internet news report flashed up on the whiteboard screen.

Explorer finds his lost treasure!

Sir Randolph Templeton Tibbs has been reunited with the wife he thought he´d lost forever.

`My wandering days are over,´ he said. `Bunty and I are going to settle down and make up for all the years we´ve been apart. The only exploring I´ll be doing from now on will be in my back garden!´

Peaches clapped her hands and cried, 'It's true! It's true!'

'Yeah! And . . . er . . .' I tried to think of something *really* rude to say, but all that came out was: 'Bobby goes moo!'

Everyone laughed, and Bobby's face went as red as Firefly, the flame-thrower man in **Agent Q and the** Hot Dogs of Hell!

I knew what he was thinking . . .

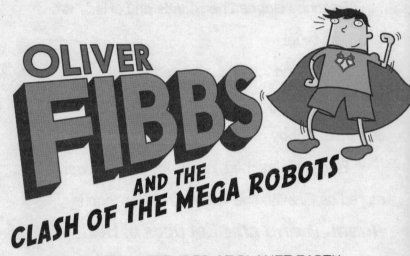